This edition published by Parragon Books Ltd in 2014

Parragon Books Ltd
Chartist House
15–17 Trim Street
Bath BA1 1HA, UK
www.parragon.com

ISBN 978-1-4723-7235-2

Printed in China

Bath • New York • Cologne • Melbourne • Delhi
Hong Kong • Shenzhen • Singapore • Amsterdam

Finn McMissile, a British secret agent, had slipped onto an oil derrick. He was spying on a spectacled criminal named Professor Z.

Finn hid in the rafters and took photos of a TV camera. He also saw another secret agent who had been crushed into scrap metal!

Back in Radiator Springs, race car Lightning McQueen was at the Wheel Well Restaurant. Miles Axlerod – a former oil tycoon – and Italian race car Francesco Bernoulli were on TV. Axlerod was hosting an international race called the World Grand Prix to introduce his new alternative fuel, Allinol. Lightning agreed to join the race.

Lightning and his pit crew soon arrived in Tokyo for the first race. Mater embarrassed Lightning at the welcome party. He even leaked oil beside Axlerod.

Mater raced off to the bathroom. Inside the automated cubicle, he got poked, prodded and splashed with water!

While Mater was in the cubicle, two members of
Professor Z's crew, Grem and Acer, roughed up
American Agent Rod "Torque" Redline. When Mater
came out of the cubicle, Torque secretly stuck a
device underneath Mater.

The following day at the racetrack, Finn and his fellow agent, Holley Shiftwell, kept a close eye on Mater. They thought he was a secret agent, too!

Nearby, Grem and Acer aimed the TV camera at a race car. The camera was a weapon! Seconds later, the car's engine exploded. Some thought Allinol was to blame.

Professor Z's gang then went after Mater in the pits. They wanted the device that the American agent had planted on him.

Just as the bad cars were closing in on Mater, Finn rushed in to the rescue. Mater thought he was watching a karate demonstration!

Since Mater was distracted, he gave Lightning bad racing tips. Lightning ended up losing the race to Francesco!

Lightning blamed Mater. "I lost the race because of you!" he exclaimed.

Mater felt so terrible he decided to go back home. But Finn and Holley whisked him off on a spy mission instead.

Holley removed the planted device from Mater and found a photo of a mysterious, gas-guzzling engine. Mater noticed it had Whitworth bolts, which were very difficult to unscrew.

Meanwhile, Lightning and his team were just outside Porto Corsa, Italy visiting Luigi and Guido's hometown. Lightning talked to Luigi's Uncle Topolino about his fight with Mater.

"Everybody fights now and then, especially best friends," said Uncle Topolino. "But you gotta make up fast."

Holley, Finn and Mater were also on their way to Porto Corsa. Mater had told them the mysterious engine belonged to a Lemon – a car that didn't work right. They soon found out that a secret meeting of Lemons was being held in Porto Corsa. Holley disguised Mater as one of the Lemons' tow trucks so he could sneak into the meeting. She also gave him lots of spy gadgets!

Mater was soon in a room with Professor Z and all the Lemons. Then their "Big Boss", whose identity was hidden, appeared on a TV screen. He told the Lemons that once Allinol was proven dangerous, all cars would go back to using gasoline. Then the Lemons, who owned most of the world's oil, would become wealthy and powerful.

Outside, the second race had begun. Grem and Acer were on a nearby tower with the camera. They aimed it at the race car from Brazil. Her engine suddenly exploded!

Finn raced to the tower to stop Grem and Acer — but a helicopter captured him with a giant magnet!

Back at the race, Lightning crossed the finish line first!
He then announced that he would still be using Allinol in
the final World Grand Prix race in London.

The Big Boss heard this and gave the order to get rid
of Lightning. Mater used his parachute to escape from the
meeting. But before he could warn Lightning, Mater was
kidnapped by the Lemons. They had captured Holley, too!

Finn, Holley and Mater were tied up inside the clockworks of Big Bentley in London. Mater finally convinced Finn and Holley that he wasn't a spy.

After the final race began, Grem and Acer told Mater they had planted a bomb inside Lightning's pit. As soon as the Lemons left, Mater escaped, racing to save his best friend.

Minutes later, Holley and Finn escaped, too. They soon discovered the Lemons had actually planted the bomb on Mater! Finn radioed the tow truck to tell him, but Mater was already in the pits.

"Stay away from me!" Mater warned Lightning.

But Lightning still raced forwards to see his best friend!

Meanwhile, Professor Z tried to escape on a combat ship, but Finn stopped him. He tied the Professor up in cables and brought him to Holley, Mater and Lightning.

Then Guido tried to remove the bomb on Mater, but he couldn't unscrew the bolts. Suddenly, everything made sense to Mater. He knew who the Big Boss was!

Mater flew with Lightning to Buckingham Palace. Mater told everyone that Axlerod was the Big Boss! Mater had figured it out because the bolts on the bomb were the same Whitworth bolts from the old British engine in the photo. The engine belonged to Axlerod. He was the biggest Lemon of all! Axlerod deactivated the bomb and everyone was saved.

The Queen thanked Mater by making him a knight!

Not long after Lightning got back home, he decided to hold his own "Radiator Springs Grand Prix". He invited all the international race cars. The whole town turned up for the race.

Finn and Holley showed up, too. They had come to invite Mater on their next mission. Mater politely turned them down. But he did take his spy gadgets for one last spin! Mater activated his rockets and blasted off down the racetrack, right beside his speedy best friend.

DISNEP · PIXAR

TOY STORY 2

When Andy arrived home from Cowboy Camp,
he was surprised by what he found. "New toys!" he cried.
"Thanks, Mum!"

Jessie and Bullseye had joined all his favourites,
welcoming him home. Andy couldn't wait to play with
everyone ... right after he sewed up Woody's shoulder!

Someday Andy would grow up and maybe he would
stop playing with toys, but Woody and Buzz knew there
was no place they'd rather be. Besides, they'd always have
each other – for infinity and beyond!

... together, they swung towards the ground!

As the two hurtled down and under the plane, Woody's pull string unhooked from the bolt on the plane – throwing them right to Buzz, who was galloping along on Bullseye! Everyone was safe.

Watching the plane take off into the sky, Woody, Jessie, Buzz and Bullseye danced and cheered.

"That was definitely Woody's finest hour!" cried Jessie.

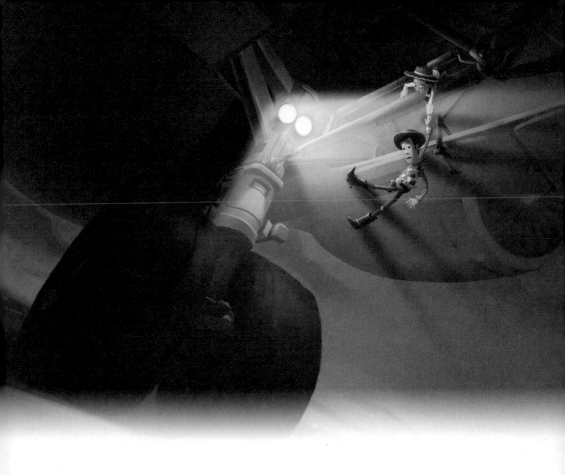

Woody quickly found the scared cowgirl.

"C'mon, Jess," he said. "It's time to take you home."

But just then, the plane's doors closed. They were stuck inside!

Desperate, they crawled through a hatch, down to the plane's wheels. The plane was already speeding down the runway. Then Woody slipped! Jessie caught him just in time, but his arm was starting to rip even more.

Twirling his pull string, Woody tried a daring trick. First he lassoed a bolt on the wheels. Then he grabbed Jessie's hand and ...

Bullseye kicked free from Al's case as the conveyor belt carried them outside, but Jessie was still stuck!

"Ride like the wind, Bullseye!" Woody yelled as he and Buzz jumped on Bullseye's back. They raced after the baggage truck. Woody finally scrambled onto the truck, but by then, the green case was already being loaded into a plane. Woody hid inside another suitcase and was tossed on to the plane, too.

Still in the pet carrier, Andy's toys climbed on to the luggage conveyer belt. Buzz finally found Al's case, but when he opened it – *POW!* – the Prospector jumped out and punched Buzz.

"Hey! No one does that to my friend," Woody yelled, tackling the Prospector.

With his pickaxe, the Prospector ripped open Woody's shoulder again. He was about to drag Woody back into the case, but Andy's toys arrived just in time to save him.

The toys couldn't walk openly through the airport, but luckily Buzz spotted a pet carrier. They piled inside, sticking their legs through the bottom so they could walk. Moving as quickly as they dared, the group followed Al and his green case.

Luckily, Buzz and the gang spotted Al leaving the building. They knew that Woody was inside his case and they had to help!

They jumped into a nearby pizza truck and, with Buzz at the steering wheel, Slinky on the pedals, Rex as navigator and Hamm working the gears, they followed Al's car all the way to the airport.

Soon, though, Woody realized that Buzz was right – he did belong with Andy! He ran to the vent and called for his friends to return. Then he turned to the *Roundup* gang. "Come with me," he said. "Andy will play with all of us, I know it!"

Jessie and Bullseye were excited ... but the Prospector blocked their path! After a lifetime in his box, he was determined to go to the museum.

Suddenly, Al returned! He packed the *Roundup* toys into a case and headed out of the door.

But Woody didn't want to leave. The *Roundup* gang needed him to make a complete set for the museum. Besides, what if Andy didn't want Woody anymore?

"You're a toy!" Buzz said. "Life's only worth living if you're being loved by a kid."

"This is my only chance," Woody protested.

Sadly, Buzz led Andy's toys towards home.

Sneaking through the air vents, the toys finally reached
Al's apartment. New Buzz rushed up to Bullseye and yelled,
"We're here, Woody!"

Andy's toys looked at the New Buzz suspiciously.
Then Andy's real Buzz appeared, having escaped the toy shelf
and caught up with the others. The toys were confused!

Finally, everyone worked out who was who. But that still
left one problem. "Woody," said the real Buzz. "We need
to leave now."

Outside, New Buzz was excited about his new mission!
He quickly led everyone into Al's apartment building
through an air vent.

"No time to lose!" he shouted.

Then, because he thought he was a real space ranger,
he tried to fly up to the top floor! Luckily, the lift came
by just in time and carried everyone up instead.

Back in Al's Toy Barn, Buzz found an aisle full of brand-new, updated Buzz Lightyear toys! He reached out to touch one of the fancy new utility belts and suddenly a hand clamped on to his wrist. It was a new Buzz Lightyear, who believed he'd caught a rogue space ranger!

New Buzz tied Old Buzz into a box and ran to join Andy's toys – and not one of them realized they'd left the real Buzz behind!

Once the toy cleaner had left, Woody told Jessie that he couldn't go to the museum, because he had to get back to Andy.

Jessie sadly explained that she had once had an owner – a wonderful little girl called Emily. But when Emily grew up, she abandoned Jessie.

"You never forget kids like Emily or Andy," said Jessie. "But they forget you."

Woody began to worry that Andy would forget about him one day, too.

Back at Al's apartment, an old man had arrived
to give Woody a makeover. The man opened a wooden
case with special trays and drawers full of toy parts
and doll paint. He cleaned Woody's eyes and ears and
repainted the top of the cowboy's head, where the paint
had worn away. He even polished Woody's boots.

Best of all, he sewed the rip in Woody's arm!

Inside Al's Toy Barn, aisles of shiny new toys
seemed to stretch into the distance. Everyone looked
up in awe – how would they ever find Woody in here?

After a long walk, the toys finally reached Al's Toy Barn. They just needed to cross one last, very busy, street.

Luckily, Buzz noticed a pile of orange traffic cones. He told everyone to grab one and then, slowly, they ventured across the street, hiding under the cones. Soon, the street was filled with skidding, honking, crashing cars, all trying to avoid the strange, moving traffic cones!

But the toys barely noticed. They had arrived at Al's Toy Barn.

Meanwhile, Buzz and the other toys had worked
out that it was Al, the owner of Al's Toy Barn, that had
taken Woody. They set out to rescue their friend.

Together, with a little help from Slinky, they jumped
off the roof.

"To Al's Toy Barn … and beyond!" Buzz cried.

Jessie turned on the television and a programme called *Woody's Roundup!* came on. It starred Jessie, Stinky Pete the Prospector, Bullseye and ... Sheriff Woody!

Woody couldn't believe it. He had once been a television star! The Prospector explained that the *Roundup* toys had become valuable collectibles. The man who had taken Woody planned to sell them all, as a set, to a Japanese museum!

The strange man took Woody to his apartment and locked
him in. Woody looked around for a way to escape.

POP! A packing box suddenly burst open and Woody was
knocked off his feet by a galloping toy horse.

"Yee-haw! It's really you!" shouted a cowgirl.

The cowgirl said she was Jessie and the horse was Bullseye.
Then she introduced the Prospector, a toy who had never been
out of his box. All of them were thrilled to see Woody!

... and stole him!

From their upstairs window, the other toys watched in horror as the man threw Woody into the boot of his car.

Buzz couldn't let Woody be taken away so easily, so he jumped out of the window and slid down the drainpipe.

But Buzz was too late – the car sped away.

Later that day, Andy's mum put on a garage sale. She came
into Andy's room and chose Wheezy as one of the sale items!

Thinking quickly, Woody waited until Andy's mum was out
of sight, then whistled for Andy's puppy. Together, they sneaked
outside, grabbed Wheezy and headed back to safety. But because
his arm was injured, Woody tumbled to the ground.

Then, a strange man noticed Woody, picked him up ...

Sadly, Andy handed Woody to his mum, who placed
the cowboy doll up on the highest shelf in the room.

Woody watched sadly as Andy left without him.
What if Andy never played with him again?

And Woody didn't feel any better when he found Wheezy,
a toy penguin, who'd been sitting broken on the shelf
for months. Maybe that would be Woody's future, too....

"Hey, Woody! Ready to go to Cowboy Camp?" Andy cried, bursting into the bedroom.

Woody was very excited about camp, though he couldn't show his feelings to Andy. Toys were supposed to stay motionless whenever people could see them.

Andy grabbed Woody and Buzz for a quick adventure. Suddenly, there was a loud *RIIIPPPP!* Woody's shoulder had ripped open!

Bath • New York • Cologne • Melbourne • Delhi
Hong Kong • Shenzhen • Singapore • Amsterdam

This edition published by Parragon Books Ltd in 2014

Parragon Books Ltd
Chartist House
15–17 Trim Street
Bath BA1 1HA, UK
www.parragon.com

ISBN 978-1-4723-7248-2

Printed in China